# ANNE AND THE
# SAND DOBBIES

*A Story about Death
for Children and Their Parents*

For

  Derek and Sheila Walson

with all best wishes

from   John and Ruth Calum

Christmas 1986

# Anne and the Sand Dobbies

JOHN B. COBURN

Morehouse-Barlow
Wilton, CT

Morehouse Barlow Co., Inc.
78 Danbury Road
Wilton, Connecticut 06897


Library of Congress Cataloging-in-Publication Data

Coburn, John B.
Anne and the sand dobbies.

Originally published: New York: Seabury Press,
1964.
Summary: A young boy related how he and his family
came to terms with the death of their young sister.
[1. Death—Fiction.  2. Brothers and sisters—
Fiction.  3. Family life—Fiction]  1. Slayton,
Sylvia, ill.  II. Title.
PZ7.C6368An     1986          [Fic]          86–12650
ISBN 0–8192–1354–3


*Printed in the United States of America*

2   4   6   8   10   9   7   5   3   1

*To* Ruth, Tom, Judy,
Mike, Sarah, *and* Cynthia

# Preface

The two most frequently asked questions by those who have read *Anne and The Sand Dobbies*—particularly children, but they probably speak for their parents as well—are, "is the story true?" and "are Sand Dobbies real?" The answer to both is, "yes."

The reason I know the story is true is because it is the story of our daughter, Cynthia Anne, who died when she was twenty months old when we were living in Newark, New Jersey. And I know the Sand Dobbies are real because they helped pull us—that is, our family—through that difficult time. We know they are real as love is real, and as wonder and imagination and enchantment are real. We learned through the death of our daughter that all life can be trusted and you better get on with it, celebrating it, kicking up your heels, diving into the waves, turning somersaults, being at times just a little bit crazy, because life is a little bit crazy. After all, what sense does it make to have your twenty-month-old sister die?

The book came to be written this way: A few weeks after Cynthia died, an editor at Seabury Press asked me if I would write a book about her death for children. I replied that that was impossible at that time but I would put it in the back of my mind and think about it. It stayed there for ten years. Then, one summer, the time seemed right. We were staying at Duneloch in Wellfleet on Cape Cod in the summer home of our friends Eli and Margaret Marsh of Amherst. Each morning I would go out to a little cabin in the pine woods, sit on the front step and write what seemed to me to recapture the events of those days. Each evening I would then read the draft of what I had written to my wife and four children. Needless to say, they did not remember everything the way I did and they were not bashful in correcting me.

"No, Pops, it wasn't that way at all. This is the way it was." You can imagine we had some brisk discussions. But they were all happy ones. We had good family times that summer recapturing as best we could the greatest trauma we had been through as a family. It was very moving—and wonderful therapy for all of us. So ten years after the invitation, I sent the manuscript off; it was accepted; *Anne and The Sand Dobbies* began to make its way into children's literature and—not so incidentally—into adults' as well. Death spares no age, and probing its mystery goes on age after age.

Now for the Sand Dobbies. Seven years before we moved

to Newark, we lived in Amherst, Massachusetts where I was the rector of the Episcopal Church and Chaplain of Amherst College. I wanted to start a lacrosse team. Initially rebuffed by the administration, I turned to the soccer coach for counsel as how best to deal with an athletic director so blind to the virtues of lacrosse.

The soccer coach was Allison (Eli) Marsh. He had for forty years been the popular and very successful coach. He had the best won-lost record of any varsity sport over those years—probably because he would say, "boys, it's only a game, just enjoy it"—and later he became athletic director himself. He responded immediately, "John, you follow my advice, get those boys out on the field, toss the ball around, let people see what you are doing, get some informal scrimmages, don't complain or criticize anybody and in four years I'll guarantee you will have an Amherst lacrosse team."

He was right. We did. He later commented, "I'll be your athletic advisor, you be my spiritual advisor." I accepted, but am quick to confess he taught me more of the life of the spirit than I ever taught him.

Well, that began a friendship with Eli and his wife Margaret which influenced our family in unexpected and wonderful ways. Eli introduced us to the Sand Dobbies and they have stayed with us ever since. Our grandchildren are now being introduced to them.

This is how we came to meet the Sand Dobbies. When Cynthia died we were not clear where her ashes should be buried. Newark was an unlikely place, so after the funeral service we decided to wait before coming to any decision. The next day our oldest child, Tom, then aged twelve, said, "I think Cynthia should be buried at the Cape. That's where we were together most as a family and besides, that's where the Sand Dobbies are."

Of course. So that summer she was buried in the little cemetery attached to the summer chapel of St. James the Fisherman in Wellfleet. Bishop James Pike, founder of the Chapel, Bishop of California, who with Mrs. Pike were godparents to Cynthia, had the service.

It was on their property on Gull Pond three years before that Eli had introduced us to the Sand Dobbies. That was before Cynthia had been born. We were renting the Pike cottage that summer. Eli and Margaret lived ten minutes away and stopped in late one afternoon to welcome us as neighbors. Eli asked us, "Want to see some Sand Dobbies?" "Certainly." So Tom, aged nine, Judy, six, and Michael, three, and I set off with him through the pine woods.

We were skirting Gull Pond as dusk was falling when Eli said, "Now you have to fall onto your stomach, crawl, and don't make a sound." We followed him, crawling on our hands

ANNE AND THE SAND DOBBIES

and knees single file, until we came nearly to the edge of the water. "What you have to do now," he said, "is close your eyes tight, press your face into the grasses and then *very slowly* lift your heads about an inch and look quickly out of the corner of your eyes.

"What will we see?" Tom asked.

"You will see little figures about an inch high," Eli replied. "They will be walking or dancing or swinging on tree branches. You will recognize them because they are unlike anything you have ever seen and yet you will sense you have known them forever. But be *very* quiet, for they are very shy."

And sure enough, that evening we saw six Sand Dobbies dancing, and life has never been the same since.

*Duneloch*                                                                                          J.B.C.
*Wellfleet, Massachusetts*
*August, 1985*

# ANNE AND THE
# SAND DOBBIES

THIS IS THE STORY about my sister, Anne, who died. It's also the story of Bonnie, my dog, who died, too—or rather he got killed. Anne and Bonnie are tied in together.

Because of them something has happened to our family, something good. How can that be good? That's what I'd like to know. That's what I'm trying to figure out and write about.

It has to do with the sand dobbies, I know that, and Mr. Field and that last summer with Anne at the beach. Somehow they helped make more sense out of it than anything else.

But I'm going to begin at the beginning with how I got my dog.

# 1

MY PARENTS don't always do what they say they'll do. Sometimes they do and sometimes they don't.

That's all right with me when they forget what I hope they'll forget—like saying "no more TV for a week" and then not doing anything about it when I go turn it on anyway.

Other times I have to keep reminding them that they promised me something just to make sure they don't forget. One thing I didn't let them forget was my dog. During last year's vacation at the beach they had promised me one for my birthday, November 8.

Every day during the fall when I got home from school I'd

remind them at suppertime, "Don't forget, folks. November 8 is coming. One dog. Nothing else. No party. No movies. No presents. No cake. No ice cream. Nothing. Just one dog. November 8. Don't forget."

Finally, after a week Mother said, "All right, Danny, we get the message. We promised you. We won't forget. One dog. November 8. Now you put it out of your mind. If you keep on like this, we'll forget it on purpose."

It's a funny thing about parents. Sometimes they drive you crazy. Other times you love them and you know you'd be lost without them. It's the same with brothers and sisters, too. At least in our family it is. One day they're great, and the next day they're awful.

Take this business of washing the car, for example. Saturday is car-washing day. Boy, do I hate it! I remember one Saturday last year just before vacation began. After breakfast

I said, "Mother, can I have my allowance for the week?" It's fifty cents.

"Have you done the car yet?" she asked. Doing the car is the way I earn the fifty cents.

"Of course he hasn't," Pete piped up. "Don't you know he hopes you'll forget he's supposed to do the car?" Pete's my older brother. He's sixteen. He sounds just like an older brother, doesn't he? And Mother knew darn well I hadn't done the car.

"Pete," I said, "why don't you shut up and mind your own business?"

"That's enough of that, boys," Mother said. "Peter, stop your teasing. Dan, you'd better get that car done before your father comes home for lunch. Maybe Sally will help you with the windows if you ask her nicely." Sally's fourteen and on the whole isn't so bad.

So just before lunch and before Dad came home, I got out the hose, the bucket, the soap, the sponge, and the towels. Mother was out in the back yard keeping an eye on Anne who was two years old.

Pete had backed the car out into the driveway and was busy shooting baskets over the garage door. As I turned on the hose, I said to him, "This sure is a miserable job. I hate it."

"There's no point complaining, buddy-boy," Pete said. "This is just part of life in this family. I hated it when I was eleven. Now you hate it."

It was then that Dad walked up the driveway. He said "hello" to us, went over and kissed Mummy, then picked up Anne and sat her on his shoulders. He walked over to the car and stood there watching me as I soaped the hood.

"There's no point getting excited about this," he said. "I

ANNE AND THE SAND DOBBIES

hated washing cars when *I* was a boy, too, but my father made me. It was a worse job then because the wheels had spokes. You just stand there with a rag and wash a hub cap with one swish. I had to wash twelve spokes on each wheel, and that was a mess, especially when they were covered with tar. My old man used to stand right over me. Believe me, I hated it."

"You mean," I asked, "that he stood over you just the way you're standing over me?"

"Don't be a wise guy, Dan. You think I'm bad. He was twice as bad as I am. When I used to complain to him—just the way you boys complain to me—he would say, 'Look, when *I* was a boy my old man used to make me curry the horse on Saturday morning. I can remember standing on that stepladder to get on top of the horse. So don't talk to me about hating work. You don't know what work is.'"

Then he continued. "Listen, boys, it's good to have some

nice family things to hate generation after generation. What do you think fathers are for, anyway? They ought to help their boys develop a few good solid hates in life. Washing cars on Saturday mornings is one of them."

Then Mother said, "Dear, that's a terrible thing to say to those boys. I don't know what gets into you sometimes."

He laughed and said, "No, I don't think you do. But I know and the boys know. Don't you, boys?" He laughed again.

I thought I understood, but I wasn't sure. Pete said, "Sure, I know. Wait until I get a boy of my own. *That* will be the day."

Then Sally came out of the house. She said, "Danny, want me to help with the windows?" From the tone of her voice I knew Mother had asked her to say this.

"I sure do," I replied. "That will be neat. Thanks very much."

"How much do I get?" she asked. "Ten cents?"

"Okay," I said. "Ten cents." That meant I would get only forty cents for myself. Boy, I thought, as I slapped one of the towels down on a fender, this is a tough way to earn a living.

That was when I decided I'd ask for a dog for my birthday. I knew my family well enough to know I'd have to pick the best time to ask them. I figured that would be sometime during vacation at the beach.

Sure enough, by the time we got back from vacation they had promised me a dog for my birthday. That was one of the greatest promises they ever kept, and that's what I want to write about now.

# 2

As IT TURNED OUT, November 8 last year came on a Saturday. The night before Dad said, "Okay, Danny, no car-washing tomorrow. That's the first birthday present. The second is the dog. We'll go out to the dog pound and see what we can find."

So after breakfast we went. I had never been to a dog pound and had always wondered what it would be like. When I was a little boy I used to think it was a place where they weighed dogs and then sold them by the pound. What it really was, of course, was just a kennel. Lost and stray dogs got put there. If nobody came to claim them, they were sold.

We drove out on the highway six miles to the dog pound, parked the car, and walked into the office. My father said to the man there, "I am the fellow that called you about the dog for a ten-year-old boy. This is the boy."

I interrupted, "I'm eleven years old, Dad, remember?"

My father said, "Yes, that's right. This is a birthday present for him. He is eleven today. Could we look at dogs?"

The man in the office was a big man. He smoked a cigar and needed a shave. "Ever own a dog?" he asked.

"No," I said, "but I have a book about dogs that shows you how to take care of a dog."

The man laughed, or maybe he just grunted, but it was a funny grunt. He kept his cigar in his mouth all the time. It had gone out, but he was chewing it anyway.

"Come on," he said, "follow me."

He took us out into the back kennel, and as soon as we

stepped out of the office, the dogs began to bark and jump and make a terrific racket. It was really kind of frightening. But the man didn't say anything. He just walked along until he came to a door.

Behind the door was a brown, medium-sized dog. He wasn't barking. He was just sitting there looking. The man opened the door, reached in, pulled him out by the scruff of the neck, and took him in his arms.

"Come on, Bonnie," he said. "Got a home for you—and a master, too."

Even though he still chewed on that cigar and was pretty fierce looking, it was nice the way he called that dog "Bonnie" and talked to him. Bonnie licked his ear, and I wondered if he liked the smell of the cigar.

It was as simple as that. Bonnie had an old collar on. The

ANNE AND THE SAND DOBBIES

man gave me a piece of rope for a leash. All he said was, "Treat him decent and he'll be decent."

Dad asked him, "What kind of a dog is he?"

The man laughed. "Who knows?" he said.

"How much does he cost?" Dad asked.

"Oh, I don't know. A dollar will do, I guess."

Dad gave him a five dollar bill. "Keep the change," he said. "Buy a box of cigars."

The man laughed again and said, "Thanks. I will."

So we got into the car and went back into town to the pet shop. There we bought a dog bed and blanket, food bowls, some dog food and vitamins, comb and brush and soap. By the time we bought everything we needed and Dad had paid the bill, he said, "Boy, if I'd known how much all this apparatus was going to cost, I'd never have given that miserable fellow five dollars."

But I think he was kidding, for he hit me on the side of the head with his hand when he said it—like he always does when he's fooling. I think he had as good a time that day as I did.

When we got home the whole family was waiting for us—Pete, Sally, Mother, and Anne. They thought Bonnie was neat. Then three of my friends came over to our backyard to see him.

One of them, Joey, asked, "What kind of a dog is he, anyway?"

I answered, "Who knows?" That was the answer that the man with the cigar at the dog pound had given my father.

Joey said, "Maybe that's what we ought to call him then—Whoknows." And he tried to get Bonnie to come to him by calling him, "Come here, Whoknows. Whoknows, come here." But Bonnie didn't pay any attention to him. Everybody liked my dog so much—especially the way he came running and wagging his tail when he was called "Bonnie"—that they felt that Bonnie was a great addition to the neighborhood.

Later I took Bonnie down cellar and showed him where he was to sleep. Then I brought down all the equipment. I put some newspapers on the floor but wasn't certain that he would know what those were for. *That* job everybody in the family pointed out to me was mine. Any mistakes I would have to take care of. I said, "Okay."

After I gave him his supper I took him out for a walk. Dad said, "Don't let him off the leash. Keep him on that leash all the time until he gets used to the neighborhood. Now, for heaven's sake, remember that—don't let him run." I said, "Okay."

Supper was great that night. Even though I had said I didn't want any birthday cake or candles or anything except the dog, Mother had made a cake for me. In the middle of the eleven candles there was a dog outlined on the frosting. Everybody even gave me a present. Anne gave me a toy dog, but got so excited she wouldn't let go of it. She just kept banging it on her high chair. We had a good time that night. It was the best birthday party I've ever had.

Bonnie whimpered a little that night, but after that he seemed right at home. He knew what the newspapers were for, too. What a smart dog! I think Pete was a little disappointed.

# 3

I'D BETTER SAY A WORD now about Anne. Anne is my sister. She *was* my sister. No, she *is* my sister. She died. I'm not sure whether she *was* or *is* my sister—maybe both.

Anyway what I'm trying to do is to tell the story about Anne. I'm trying to figure out what has happened to her.

The thing is I can't tell about Anne without telling about Bonnie, too. They're tied in together. They are in my mind anyway, and I hope they really are.

What's the point of having a dog if he can't be yours forever? And what's the point of having a sister if she can't be yours forever, too? What's the point of having a dog and a sister together if they can't always be together? So, when I tell the story about Anne, I keep thinking of Bonnie, too. And I keep thinking of Anne at the beach because that was where I saw her most of the time.

We have a house there. It is out in the woods in the middle of pine trees on the edge of a fresh-water lake and only half a mile from the ocean. Ever since I can remember, the family has gone there for the whole summer, except for Dad who is usually there just for August.

Anne was two years old last summer. She never talked, of course. At least she never talked so you could understand her. Mother pretended she could, but I don't think she really did. She used to chirp—especially when she was happy, and that seemed to be almost all the time. That was about the only sound that came out of her, except for crying once in a while, but never for long.

Even when nobody was around she would make little chirping sounds to herself. Mother used to put her out in the sandpile under the trees. Actually, it wasn't a real sandpile. The sand just happened to be there. It was everywhere. Dad simply nailed some chicken wire around the trees, and Anne had a playpen.

Sometimes when I was left in charge of her, I'd crawl along the outside of the fence on my stomach and growl at her or bark. She'd chirp back. Then she'd crawl over and reach through the chicken wire, pull my hair, and laugh.

Other times I'd sit back among the trees and watch her. She'd sit up straight and look out over the water. She seemed to keep looking at something 'way over on the other shore. She'd chirp and then she'd stop. There was a row of trees in the distance on the horzion. You'd think she was waiting to hear what the trees—or some spirit or whatever it was she

was talking to—would say to her. You felt somehow that she was living in another world, that something in that other world was speaking to her, and still she was here in this world.

I used to climb into her pen once in a while and lie on my back. I'd pull my knees up. She'd sit up there and jump up and down on my stomach. Then I'd put her on my feet while I was still lying down, stick my feet up in the air, hold her hands and jiggle her gently. That was when you had a chance to look up at the sky through the pine trees and through her hair. I used to think, "That's really pretty."

Sometimes she would climb on my back, and I'd crawl on my hands and knees out into the pine trees. There we'd just sit and not make a move and listen. Some days when there was no wind and everything was dead still—especially on real hot days when there wasn't a single sound—it seemed almost as though the whole earth stood still. You wondered if it had stopped spinning and if this meant you and everything else were going to slide off.

Then if you'd wait long enough, the breeze would come up. Just a little breath of air sometimes, but you'd hear the wind in the distance. One minute you'd see the leaves bobbing softly up and down, and you'd know the wind was right near you, even though you couldn't feel it. It would just come. You'd hear the wind go through the branches and you'd ask yourself, "I wonder how this tree likes feeling the wind?" Then it would go and everything was dead still again. Every once in a while Anne would let out that little gentle chirp.

I'd sit with my back to one of the trees and take a deep breath. Then I'd press back against the tree and think, "I wonder what it's like just to be a tree?" After I'd held my breath as long as I could, I'd scoop Anne up in my arms, and we'd roll over and over on the moss. Then the chirps became gurgles of laughing, and we'd tear back to the house.

Sometimes early in the evening after she'd had her supper, I used to put her on my shoulders and walk down the back dirt road to the crossroads, then along a path down into a little hollow where three paths crossed. It was like a fork in the road, but in the middle of that fork there were about a dozen pine trees. They made a kind of little grove.

That was where the sand dobbies played. It was a magic place where they used to come at night sometimes and dance. I wanted to see if Anne could see them. I hoped she could. I had seen them a few times when I was just a little boy. At least I think I could remember seeing them. As a matter of fact everybody in our family had seen them at one time or another. They all said they had.

The man who introduced us to them was Mr. Field. He was an old friend of Daddy and Mummy's. He lived at the beach most of the year. The first thing I remember about him was one day when Dad and I were walking along the sand dunes we saw somebody in the distance galloping along on a horse. He was going like the wind.

"Look, Danny," Dad said. "Look at that beautiful sight." And it was the most beautiful thing I had ever seen in my life. It seemed as though the horse were going ninety miles an hour, with his neck stretched out in front and his tail streaming out in back. It was a wild-looking thing. And there was somebody on his back.

"It's Mr. Field," Dad said. "I recognize his horse. Maybe he'll see us."

He whistled as loud as he could and waved his arms. He called, "Fieldy, Fieldy, come over here."

Sure enough he did see us. He came toward us, slowed down to a trot, and drew the horse to a halt. He jumped off, and I saw that he was riding bareback.

"Fieldy," Dad said. "Where are you going?"

"Going?" said Mr. Field. "Why, I'm going to take the temperature of the water in the ocean." All he had on was a pair of shorts.

"Where's your thermometer?" Dad asked him.

"Thermometer?" he said. "I don't need a thermometer. I use my left ankle." I looked at his left ankle. He shook it.

"See," he said. "That's just as good as any old mercury tube. I have mercury in that ankle. When I dip it in the water it tells the temperature, and I'm never off by more than one degree."

That was my introduction to Mr. Field. He became a good friend. He used to let me ride in front of him on the horse, and while we never went as fast as that first time I saw him, we did get to gallop over the sand dunes.

He knew the names of all the birds in the woods. He fed and finally tamed a whole family of quail. He loved the out-of-doors and everything in it.

"I leave here during hunting season, Danny," he said once. "Men come down here from the cities for a whole week with their guns. They come to kill deer. They walk all over my property, pay no attention to "Keep Off" signs, and then they kill my friends, the deer, who live with us. I can't stand it, so Mrs. Field and I just leave. We don't come back till the spring-time."

I liked Mr. Field for that. But I loved him because he was the one who introduced me to the sand dobbies.

# 4

As a matter of fact, Mr. Field introduced all the members of our family to the sand dobbies. I can't remember when they weren't part of our life at the Cape, but I was never quite sure about them until one summer when I must have been five or six years old. Then it came my turn to meet them.

Mr. Field came to our cottage late one afternoon.

"Danny," he said, "tell your pa you're going out with me to see some sand dobbies."

"Sand dobbies?" I asked. "What's that?"

"It's not, 'What's that?'" he replied. "It is, 'Who are they?'"

"Well, all right. Who are they?"

"I'm not going to tell you. I'm going to show you. Now go tell your family you're off to see sand dobbies."

Everybody was out on the beach, so when I told them what Mr. Field had said, Pete replied, "Say, that's great. I love sand dobbies. I'm going, too."

"No, you're not, young man," Dad said. "You're not invited. This is not your party."

"That's right, Pete," said Sally. "Let Danny go by himself."

"Good luck, Dan," said Dad. "You go ahead, and tell us about them when you get back."

So Mr. Field and I walked down the road to this little grove where I later took Anne.

As we came closer, he said, "Danny, we have to whisper from now on." He dropped his voice. "The less noise the better."

When we were still a little way from the crossroads, he

whispered, "It's best here to get off the road and go through the woods on our hands and knees."

So I followed him, both of us crawling on the moss under the pine trees. Soon he stopped where you could look down into a little hollow. He stretched out on his stomach. I did the same.

He said, "We'll wait here. The sun hasn't quite set yet. We have to wait until it gets a little shadowy in here."

I noticed the sunlight shining through the trees. It was very quiet. Slowly the light faded down below us. It seemed almost dark there.

"Now," said Mr. Field, "you keep your eyes peeled and watch around the base of those trees. Pretty soon you'll see something."

"What will I look for?" I asked.

"You just wait. You'll find out."

It was getting kind of scary. I was glad Mr. Field was there. I felt safe with him.

Suddenly he whispered, "There, there's one. See him?"

I looked. I saw something move. At least I thought I did.

"There. There's another," said Mr. Field. "Oh, Danny, this is going to be a good night. They must like you. It's not often they let you see so many the first time here."

I looked again. Something *did* seem to be moving. Why, the whole ground under those trees seemed to be going slowly up and down, not evenly, but in little quick jerks.

"Look at that," he said. "See what lovely little fellows they are. Don't they have a good time, though? Why, I do believe they're going to dance for us." He paused.

"Yes, they are. My heavens, Danny, this is wonderful. Look at them hold hands. And now some have climbed up in the branches of the trees. Look at those old fellows up there.

ANNE AND THE SAND DOBBIES

They're probably too old to dance. Or maybe they're too young. It's hard to tell the age of sand dobbies. They look young and old and wise and impish all at the same time. Do you see them, Dan, up there?"

I looked again. I did see them. I did. I was sure I did. "Yes," I said. "I see them. Little fellows they are!"

"What color, Danny?"

I blinked. "Green, I think. I think green, maybe yellow."

"Yes, that's right. Usually green, sometimes yellow, though. Most often green on their bodies, and those little things like ears that stick up are usually yellow. But, of course, you never can be sure."

I looked as hard as I could. I did see them. I was sure I did. So we sat quietly. I looked away just for a moment. The sunlight had now gone completely.

ANNE AND THE SAND DOBBIES

When I looked back, Mr. Field stood up and said, "There. They've gone. Too bad. They just skip out of there in a second. I always wonder how they do it.

"That was fine, Danny," he said, turning to me. "It's not often that they stay as long as that. You have to look very quickly most of the time to see them. Sometimes they come and go just in a flash. There are some people who say you can see them best out of the corner of your eye, that if you look at them straight on, they get frightened and disappear. But I don't think that's right. What do you think, Danny?"

He stood up and took hold of my hand, as we walked along the path and out into the road turning back toward the house.

"Gee, I don't know," I answered. "It was so quick, and the light was bad. But they were great. They give you a funny feeling, don't they?"

"You're right, Dan. They do something to you and they do something for you. Thanks, Dan, for coming with me. We'll do it again sometime," he said.

"Thank you, Mr. Field," I said.

That night, just before I went to sleep, Dad told me some more about the sand dobbies and Mr. Field. Dad said it had taken Mr. Field years of living there quietly in the woods before the sand dobbies would trust him. At first he could see them at a distance, but when he came closer, they all ran away and disappeared in the dark. Later he would go down and sit in the woods not far from where we were that afternoon. The sand dobbies then began to get used to him and finally even came to trust him. At last they would let him come down and watch them while they danced.

Mr. Field told Dad he was waiting for the day when the

sand dobbies would invite him to dance with them. "That," he said, "will be heaven."

Some people say they don't believe there is any such thing as a sand dobby. They just don't know. Mr. Field has even painted one of the sand-dobby dances. The painting is hanging in his living room, and it is a picture of that very same grove where I would carry Anne. You can even recognize the trees. Some sand dobbies are sitting in the branches of the trees, and others are holding hands dancing around the middle. They all are having a good time.

People sometimes ask what sand dobbies are like. I tell them they are something like elves or fairies. They are about three inches high. And they are sort of a mixture of green and brown and yellow.

Some people say, "Fairies or elves don't exist. They are only make-believe."

And then I say, "Well, these elves aren't make-believe. They're real."

The trouble is you can't go around talking about sand dobbies with just anybody. You have to be a special kind of person or belong to a special kind of family to understand about sand dobbies.

Mr. Field said one day, "You belong to a good sand-dobby family, Dan. Everybody in your family knows about sand dobbies. But children best of all. The younger the better. Five is a good age. Four sometimes. It's always easier to see sand dobbies with a child. But once you've seen them, you never forget them. Even your father and mother are pretty good with sand dobbies. It's a good family you belong to, Danny."

So that's really why I used to take Anne down to the grove last summer—to see if she could see them. I guess I figured if anybody could see elves or fairies, Anne ought to be able to. She seemed to be in touch with something a little unreal anyway, but I really don't know whether she ever saw them or not. She never seemed to think those trees were any greater than any other trees.

I think the trouble was that she thought that *all* trees were great. Because everything was so great all the time, there wasn't anything greater about those trees than any others. My guess is that the sand-dobby world was more real to her than the real world. Rather, that the sand-dobby world and the real world were for her all mixed in together. Anyway, down there in that grove I would tell her about the sand dobbies, and she'd chirp and pull my hair. That's what I think was real neat.

One evening when I came back with her from one of these trips and walked into the living room Pete said, "Well, Danny boy, did you show her the sand dobbies? What did she do?

Dance with them? Did she jump for joy? Or did you scare them all away for her?"

"Shut your big mouth," I said.

Sally chipped in, "Come here, Anne. Let me comb those sand dobbies out of your hair."

"Leave her alone, Sally," I cried. "And mind your own business."

Mother said, "All right, children, that's enough of that. Pete, I'm not going to have any more of that teasing. Dan, watch your language. Sally, you know better than to make fun of your brother. You were his age once."

Well, except for the last part, this is what I remember most about my sister, Anne. She and the sand dobbies understood each other and belonged to each other in a world all their own.

# 5

BONNIE WAS MY DOG all right. There wasn't any question about that. Except when I was at school I was with him all the time.

I fed him. I combed him every night, took the ticks out and put them in a jar of alcohol. I washed him. At first I washed him every day. Then at the end of the first week Dad said I couldn't wash him again for a month. I found out later that twice a year was enough—even Dad didn't know that. I took him for walks first thing in the morning and last thing at night, before school and right after school. Two or three times I had to clean up after him. Even that wasn't so bad.

Anybody has a right to be sick once in a while and make a mistake.

The person he was with most, except for me, was Anne. Mother said that she didn't have to spend nearly as much time taking care of Anne now that Bonnie had arrived.

She would put them both out in the backyard where Dad had put some more chicken wire between the house and the garage, making a pen for Bonnie as well as for Anne. Anne would hold on to the scruff of Bonnie's neck and walk around and around the pen. Then when she grew tired and sat down, Bonnie would curl up beside her. There she would chirp her little noises, and Bonnie would blink back. Anne would pull his ears, bury her face in his side, and love him.

As a matter of fact, the whole family loved Bonnie. Even Sally thought that he was nice and a real addition to the family, and for a girl that was something.

The only person who caused me any trouble was Pete. One afternoon when he came in from his newspaper route and saw me about ready to take Bonnie for a walk, he turned to Dad, who had just driven in the driveway from work, and said so I could hear him, "This is a fine thing all right. How come Danny gets a dog? I never had a dog when I was his age. I don't see why Danny gets all the breaks, and I don't get any of them."

"You're crazy," I said. "You know darn well that you've had just as many things as I have. You have a lot more. I've never had a bicycle of my own, or a sled. All I get are your hand-me-downs. You beat them all up, and then when you're through with them or outgrow them, I get them. This is the first time that I've ever had anything my own, brand-new— and even he isn't brand-new. He's a secondhand dog. Not that I care about that, though."

ANNE AND THE SAND DOBBIES

Dad interrupted, "Now you two boys just stop arguing. That's a very childish way for you to talk, both of you. Especially you, Pete. You're old enough to know that what you say simply isn't true. And as for you, Dan, you ought to be a little bit more generous with that dog than you have been. Why don't you let Pete take him for a walk once in a while? You don't have to monopolize him all the time."

"All right," I said. I knew I couldn't win the battle with Dad right there. "Here, Pete, take the leash." Pete took the leash.

"Now, Pete," I said, "hold the leash in your left hand. You walk on the sidewalk. Have Bonnie walk on your left side, and keep him on the grass. When you get down to the end of the block, turn around and have him come up on the other side, still on the grass. If you want to, on the way back see if you can make him heel. When you do that, shorten the leash and keep him by your heel and say 'Heel.' It goes better if you trot a little."

Pete set off down the sidewalk and came to the end of the block. Before he started back, I heard him say to Bonnie, "Now, Bonnie, sit. That's a good dog. Sit." Bonnie sat. Pete patted him.

"Now," he said, "let's see you roll over. Roll over, Bonnie, roll over. Come on now, roll over." Bonnie just kept on sitting.

I looked up at Dad. "You see what happens when I let Pete take the dog. He never can be content just to do what I ask him to do. He always has to go you one better. Poor Bonnie, I'll bet he's saying, 'O Master, let me walk with thee.'"

Dad laughed and said, "Well, Dan, I'm glad to see you've got some religion. It's not much but it's something. I guess we ought to be thankful for that. Now, for heaven's sake, let Pete play with the dog for a little while."

He turned and went into the house. I heard him laugh again and say to Mother, "Jean, do you want to hear something?" But I never did hear what he had to say.

# 6

THE NEXT THING THAT HAPPENED was that Anne got sick.

At first she just had a temperature. The doctor came and said it was a virus and for her to take some medicine, and if in a couple of days the temperature didn't go down, he would be back.

In a couple of days the temperature didn't go down. The doctor came back and said, "Keep her on this medicine. Her temperature will go down. Keep me in touch." Then she got better.

When she got better, Mother got sick. They had to take her to the hospital. I don't know what the trouble was, but

Dad did say that the doctor told him, "We might just as well get it done first as last." Since Anne was better they decided this was the time for her to go.

She seemed to be gone an awful long time. Maybe it was because with her away Pete and Sally became bosses around the house—except when Dad was home, which wasn't very often. They kept saying, "Mother would want you to do this" or "Mother would want you to do that"—like picking up my room, cleaning off the table after supper, straightening out the downstairs closet. I knew darn well that Mother wouldn't want any of that stuff as much as they insisted.

What was worse was that during Mother's second week in the hospital Anne got sick again.

I remember Dad calling the doctor to tell him. When he hung up he turned to me and said, "Dan, you be a good egg and take Bonnie down to the drugstore and get that prescription filled again, will you?"

I said, "Sure." Bonnie and I went to the drugstore where I picked up the prescription and brought it back home. I also bought some ice cream for supper. Sally said it would dress up the meal. I thought most of the meals needed some dressing up all right. They were pretty skimpy while Mother was gone.

During the day Mrs. Smith, who had done some babysitting for us and was a practical nurse, came in to take care of Anne while we kids were at school and Dad was at work. She would leave every day at five o'clock.

We each got our own breakfast, which, since Mother wasn't around to prepare anything, meant cold cereal. Sally and Dad would make the suppers. Usually they were either hamburgers or more cold cereal.

I complained one night, "I love cold cereal in the morning, Sally, but I don't see why I have to have it morning and night. I don't think much of this for a meal at suppertime."

Dad interrupted. "Now there's nothing the matter with cold cereal for supper. It reminds me of when I was a little boy. I used to have cold cereal lots of times. Cold cereal with hot milk, as a matter of fact."

Pete said, "That sounds just awful."

"And sometimes not even cereal," went on Dad, "but just bread and hot milk."

Pete commented, "That sounds even worse."

Then he turned to Dad and said, "Well, it may be Okay for you to be reminded of your childhood but why do *we* have to be reminded of it?"

"Now don't be a wise guy, Pete," said Dad. "I don't care if you're reminded of my childhood or not. All I want you to do is eat the cold cereal. Just be thankful I don't insist you make the milk hot."

It seemed to me Dad was getting edgy along with all the rest of us with Mummy away. The next afternoon when he came home, he said, "Never mind about supper here tonight, kids. We'll go out and have a good meal in a restaurant. I have asked Mrs. Smith to come back for the evening." When she came in, he told her that the next time for Anne to take her medicine was seven o'clock.

As we were leaving Mrs. Smith said to Dad, "Now don't you worry. I'll take care of Anne. You and the children go off and have a good time."

We went downtown to a restaurant where Dad said, "All right, chickens, you can have anything you want. What'll it be?"

Sally said, "I'd like a hamburger."

ANNE AND THE SAND DOBBIES

Dad said, "That's foolish. You can get hamburger at home anytime you want to. Order something special."

"No," said Sally, "I *like* hamburgers. If I can have anything I want, then that's what I want."

"Okay," said Dad, "have it your own way. What are you going to have, Pete?"

"Why, I think I'll have cold cereal, Dad—cold cereal with hot milk."

"What are you trying to do, wise guy, kid me? You can't have cold cereal—not even with hot milk."

"Oh, come on, Dad. Let me have some cold cereal. Just a little cold cereal with lots of hot milk. Like Granddad used to make."

"He didn't make it, Pete. I made it. He wouldn't touch the stuff himself. He made me eat it."

"Say, Dad, do you think your father was harder on you than you are on us?"

"I know perfectly well he was. You don't know what it is to have a difficult father. He used to say to me, 'The trouble with you, son, is that you don't know what work is.'"

"Seems to me I can remember hearing the same words myself. Is that where you learned them, Dad?"

"You go to the devil, young man. And stop kidding your old man. I'll do the ordering around here."

He turned to the waiter. "Waiter," he said, "this boy will have steak. So will the other one. So will I. Medium rare. Sally, are you sure you won't change your mind?"

"No," said Sally, "I love hamburger."

"All right, Sally, if that's what your little heart desires, that's what you shall have."

All in all it was a good meal.

When we came back home, Dad asked Mrs. Smith, "How did she seem?"

She said, "Well, I've seen sicker children, but I'm not very happy about how she is. I hope the doctor will come around and see her again tomorrow."

Dad said, "Well, if her temperature hasn't gone down by morning, I'll call him before I go to work. Thank you for coming. We had a good time."

Before we trooped off to our rooms we all went in for a minute to take a look at Anne. She was in her crib. She looked warm, but not as blistering hot as she had the week before, and her breathing wasn't as noisy as it had been. So we all patted her on the head, said "good night" and went to bed.

The next morning was kind of weird. Something seemed to have happened to Dad overnight. It was strange. He looked pale, as though he had been sick himself, although he was just as nice and gentle and polite as he could be. He said he hoped that we'd be careful on our way to school.

"Don't forget," he said. "Put on your boots and gloves and mufflers so you will be warm enough." He reminded us "to watch out crossing the streets and be sure to obey the lights." He hadn't done that in years. Then he said he certainly would be glad to see us later in the day, and we'd all have an evening together.

This wasn't like him at all. Usually he kids us, but he never makes any fuss about what we are going to wear or whether we are going to be warm enough. That was Mother's job. She was good at it, too.

On the way to school I said to Sally, "What's the matter with Dad, anyhow? He's never been this fussy before."

Sally replied, "I think he's just plain worried about

Mother. He's not much use around the house anyway, and he knows it. Anne's being sick has just made it all the worse."

Pete piped up, "That's right. Besides, I don't think he had much sleep last night. I heard him going up and down stairs a couple of times. Once I thought he was talking to somebody on the telephone, and another time I would have sworn that I heard the doorbell ring. I know he's upset. Even when he said just now at breakfast that Anne seemed to be a little bit better, he didn't act as though he believed it himself—almost as though he didn't really care."

Things went along as usual in school that morning until the beginning of the last period. After the bell for the changing of classes at 11:20, my homeroom teacher came down to my desk and said I was wanted in the principal's office.

That scared me. I'd been there once before when I'd had

a fight during recess with Joe Hughes. The reason for that was that Joe had let the air out of the tires on my bike. The principal had said, "It doesn't make any difference what the reason is. There is no excuse for fighting in the schoolyard at any time. If you're back in here again for any reason like this, you're going to be in serious trouble, and I will have to call your father."

On my way to the office I wondered what I'd done now. I couldn't think of anything particularly bad—at least around school.

The principal was in the doorway and greeted me. He was obviously waiting for me. "Danny," he said, "your father is here." Suddenly I had a sinking feeling in the pit of my stomach. Something was wrong.

"Gosh," I thought, "now what have I done? It must be serious to have Dad here."

I went into the office and there he was. Sally and Pete were standing there beside him. Dad said to the principal, "Thank you very much for your understanding. They'll be back in a few days."

Then turning to us he said, "Okay, kids, get your coats. Let's go. We're going home."

We went out to the car. He said, "Dan, you get in the front seat next to me. You other two get in the back." We got in.

He shut the door on his side. He didn't start the motor. Instead, he turned sideways in his seat and looked at us. Then he said, "I'm sorry to pull you out of school like this, but something terrible has happened and we've got to be together. You see, Anne died last night."

He stopped. I could see him swallow hard. He went on. "She just stopped breathing after you children had gone to bed right before midnight. I had to tell your mother first, so

I've just been to the hospital. She said that she was going to come home no matter what the doctors said, so I talked to the doctors and they said 'of course she should go home.' As a matter of fact, Anne's doctor is bringing her back to the house now. She ought to be there by the time we get back."

Then he did something he didn't often do. He put out his hand and touched each one of us gently alongside the cheek. "I'm sorry, kiddos," he said, and he swallowed hard some more.

Pete said, "Golly, Dad, we all are. We all are."

Sally said, "Why, that's just awful. Why, this is just awful. Just awful. Poor Anne."

I didn't say anything for a minute. But after the car got started and we were on our way back home, I turned to Dad and said, "Dad, why did God kill her?"

He kept looking straight ahead for a minute. Then he

turned to me and said, "That's a good question, son. A good question."

I looked hard at him. The question somehow seemed to make him feel better. He let out his breath, and he nearly smiled.

"Well," he said finally, "I don't think God killed her. We'll see." Then he stopped again. He looked almost relieved.

He said again, "That's a good question, Dan. A good question."

I didn't think it was such a good question. I wanted to know—why would God kill Anne?

# 7

IT SURE WAS A RELIEF to see Mother. She was propped up in her bed, and it was just plain wonderful to have her back. When we came into the room she burst into tears, then kissed us. Then Sally and I cried, too. Pete didn't cry. Dad didn't cry. They sniffled an awful lot, though. Dad walked out of the room very quickly several times. We'd hear him blow his nose and then he'd come back again.

Anyway, the three of us kids sat on Dad's bed. Dad sat on the bottom of Mother's. He told us the story of what had happened.

"I gave Anne the medicine at eleven o'clock right on

schedule. She seemed about the same, except her fever wasn't raging the way it had been a week ago. I thought she seemed a little bit more comfortable. I went to bed, but I couldn't sleep. After awhile I got up and tiptoed into her room. I didn't want to waken her by turning on the light so I just listened. Remember how she wheezed when she breathed? Well, I couldn't hear anything. I touched her. I picked up her hand and it was cold. She wasn't breathing. There wasn't a sound. It was that dreadful, awful silence that hit me. I knew then she had died. It was as simple as that. As terrible as that.

"I called the doctor and said, 'Anne is dead. You'd better come over.'"

"He said, 'Oh, she can't be. I'll be right over.' I looked at the clock. It was a quarter to twelve.

"Well, he came over. He went in to see Anne. I had already touched her in the dark, but I didn't want to go in and just look at her. He came downstairs after a few minutes and said, 'It must have been a sudden filling up of the lungs. Sometimes it happens like this with little children. We don't yet seem to be able to control it the way we should. It's very sudden. I remember once,' he went on, 'I had a trained nurse on a case with a little boy just Anne's age. He had the same kind of a virus infection in the upper respiratory tract. The nurse had given him the medicine and had tucked him into his crib. She turned around to get another blanket. When she turned back again, the baby was dead. That's how fast and unexpectedly it can happen.'

"There wasn't much else he could say. He is a fine fellow and a fine doctor. Obviously he was just as upset as he could be. I know he did everything the way he thinks it should have been.

ANNE AND THE SAND DOBBIES

"I guess we talked for a half hour or so. I warmed up some leftover coffee.

"Then I said to him, 'Well, there's no point in ruining the whole night for you. You'd better go and get some sleep.'

"'What about an undertaker?' he asked. 'Why don't you let me call one? I'll get him over here right away and then I'll go.'

"'That would be fine,' I said. Suddenly I thought about all the arrangements that would have to be made. I didn't see any point in having you involved in all that business of moving Anne's body.

"I was sorry to have to lie to you this morning, kids, and I was afraid you, Sally, in particular might want to take a peek into Anne's room before you left for school. I figured I'd try to get you off to school just as though nothing had happened.

Then I'd go down the first thing to tell your mother and we'd see where we'd go from there.

"Anyway, the doctor called the undertaker and in about half an hour two men had come, gone upstairs, carried Anne down and taken her back to their place. We talked a little bit longer. Then I told him he really ought to go home and get some sleep. So I thanked him for all he had done and he left.

"The strange thing," he said, "is that I really wanted to be alone. I didn't want to talk any more. I wanted to think.

"I remember picking up Pete's baseball bat from the hall closet. And I walked around the living room swinging it like a golf club. Then I lifted it to my shoulder as though it were a rifle and I sighted along it. I pointed it through the window to the darkness outside. And there it was, aimed right at blackness, and you couldn't see a thing.

"Then I thought, 'Brother, this is it. This is what it's all about. There is no neat light in that darkness. It's just plain dark. Now it's up to you! What are you going to do?'

"I pulled the trigger. And right away I felt better, as though I had just that minute been let in on a big secret. In fact, *the* big secret. Now, you figure that one out, will you, kiddos?

"All right," he finished. "Now let's get on with our business."

He turned to Mummy. "I hadn't expected you to come home, Jean, but I must say I'm glad that you insisted on it. Thank the good Lord the operation was successful enough so that you could be here. So now we're all here, and we've got to decide what we're going to do."

"Who knows about Anne?" Mummy asked.

"Nobody," said Dad, "except the doctors and the undertakers—and the principal of the school. We'll have to call our families, of course, but there's no point in doing that until we can tell them what we're going to do. The first thing we've got to do is to plan on some kind of a funeral service. Today's Tuesday. We ought to have the service on Friday."

Pete asked, "Why wait three days? Can't we have the funeral tomorrow and get it over with?"

"No," Dad said, "three days is the custom and besides, your mother's going to need three days to get her strength back a little bit—that is," he said, turning to Mother, "if you're going to the funeral. Maybe it would be better for you not to go."

"Of course I'm going to the funeral. We're all going to go."

Sally said, "I've never been to a funeral. What do we do there?" I hadn't been to one either and wondered myself what one was like. Pete said he'd been once, but couldn't remember much about it except he didn't like it.

Mummy said, "Well, you don't do anything except go

there. There is no reason not to like it if it's a service for someone you love. The minister reads from the Bible and says some prayers. Then we sing some hymns."

"What hymns do we sing?" I asked.

"Oh, I don't know," Mummy said, "we'll work that out with the minister. The only thing I'm going to insist on is that there be some cheerful hymns."

Pete asked, "How about that one for children, 'I sing a song of the saints of God'?"

Mummy said, "That's a nice one for children. I like it, too. What do you think about it?" she said, turning to Dad.

"You know perfectly well what I think about it. I think it's a corny hymn. But this is a family affair, and if this is what everybody else wants, we'll have it. Whatever goes on from now on is going to be something that we all decide on together."

Then Mother asked, "She's going to be cremated, isn't she?"

"Cremated?" Sally asked. "Isn't that when you burn the body? Are we going to cremate Anne?"

"We certainly are," put in Mother. "We're not going to go through that whole business of making such a to-do about her body as though she were still in it. What is important is Anne—not her body. Her body now has nothing to do with Anne. It's just that she once lived in it, but she isn't there now."

"Well, if she isn't there, where is she?" I asked.

"She can't be *there*," Dad said, "because she died. That is, her body died. She isn't in that body anymore. From our point of view it doesn't make any difference what happens to her body. It was hers once. That is where she lived. She brought life to it. All we want to do, really, is to honor Anne by taking some care of her body. We pay our respects. Her body is where Anne once lived, but now she has outgrown it. But don't think for a minute that that's where Anne is. She isn't."

"Are you going to burn her heart, too, Dad?" I asked.

"Dan," Dad turned to me, "what do you mean 'am I going to burn her heart, too?' *I'm* not going to burn anything. This is just something that is done. Yes, her heart is going to be burned along with her body. Her heart stopped. There isn't anything of Anne's there now. When your body dies, all of you dies."

"Well," I said again, "if Anne isn't there in her body, where is she?"

"Well, Dan, that's a good question. That's another good question. That's two in one morning. We'll talk about this lots of times," Dad said. "The simplest way to put it, I guess, is to say she's with God. Some people say she's in heaven. I don't know exactly *where* she is. All we know is that she is living and she's all right—wherever she is."

"Golly," Pete said. "I miss her already."

"Of course you do," Dad said. "We all miss her. We'll always miss her. It's awful for her to die," he went on. "There's nothing nice about it. Even if she is all right wherever she is now with God, we still miss her. But we miss her for ourselves. It is our loss. She probably is even better off."

Pete said, "How could she be better off?"

Dad said, "No, I won't say that. I'm not sure of that. She would have enjoyed living. We loved having her. Our life was better because of hers. I think maybe it's not too much to say even that her life was better because of us. So I'll take that back. We'll have to leave that open."

He went on. "Let's leave it for a minute like this: She's

with God. She is Okay. We'll talk more about this later on, but right now we've got to get on with the practical questions."

"Yes," Mother said. Then turning to Dad, she said, "Darling, why don't you call the minister? Tell him what happened. Ask him if we can have the service on Friday, let's say at two o'clock. Let's get that settled anyway."

Dad went out and made the telephone call and in a few minutes came back and said, "That's all right. We're all set. Now, do you want me to call anybody and tell them about it?"

Mummy said, "No, not right now. Let's wait. We can at least take a little time now to figure out things for ourselves, and then we'll let people know."

Pete asked, "Dad, what are you going to do with the ashes after you get them?"

Dad said, "I don't know. We'll have to decide about that. What do you think, Jean? Do you have any ideas?"

"No. In some cemetery, I suppose. Oh heavens, what are we going to do about that?" she went on. "Are we going to use the cemetery here? Suppose we move away. We probably will sometime. I don't think we're going to spend the rest of our lives here. Is this the cemetery where we ought to put Anne? Do we want to leave her here all by herself?"

Pete said, "I thought you said she wasn't here any more, Mummy?"

"Well, she isn't really. That is, she is and she isn't. She isn't here in the body. I know that. We all know it. Yet what is left of her here we want to take care of as well as we can. We don't want to just make believe that what's left doesn't make any difference at all. Her ashes—and the burying of them—sort of give us a reminder so that we can think of her. That's all."

"Well," said Dad, "if we're not going to put the ashes in the cemetery here, were are we going to put them? We've got to do something with them."

"Why don't we just scatter them?" Pete asked. "You can scatter ashes, can't you? I've read about where some people scatter ashes from airplanes or ships."

"Sure you can," answered Dad. "There's no reason at all why we can't do that. Lots of times people have their ashes scattered near places they've loved. One of my college friends scattered his father's ashes over a trout stream where they'd fished since he was a little boy."

He turned to Mummy, "What about this idea, Jean? What do you think?"

"Well, I don't know," she answered. "I don't suppose there is any reason why we can't do that. I would like, though—I *think* I would like—some special place where we could think of her particularly rather than just scattered in general to the winds or to the ocean.

"Anyway, we don't have to decide now. We can just get through the funeral and then make up our minds later about the ashes. I'm sure the undertaker can keep them. Though," she added, "I hate to think of Anne's ashes just sitting in the undertaker's office until we make up our minds. But I do know I don't want them put in the cemetery here."

Pete said, "Well, why can't we put the ashes someplace down near the beach where we are in the summer and where we'll be every summer?"

"Gee," I said, "I think that's neat."

"Perfect," said Sally, "just perfect."

Dad said, "What do you think, Jean?"

Mummy said, "I think that's just a wonderful idea. That's

where we are as a family. It's where the children played most with Anne. It's where we all have our happiest times together. Oh, Pete, thank you for that idea."

Dad said, "There, that's settled. Thanks, Pete, old bean."

Then everybody seemed quite relieved after that. The worst somehow seemed to be over. Dad said to Mummy, "Well, I suppose we'd better sit down and make a list of people we should call on the phone."

Mummy said, "All right, but first I think it would be nice before we get involved with everybody else if we could just have a little prayer here."

Our family prayers usually were pretty hectic. We all either giggled or had fights or just got bored. When they got awful, Dad would say, "All right. No more of this nonsense. If you can't behave yourselves we'll stop saying prayers."

So we'd stop for a few days or a week or a month. Then either Mummy or Dad would say, "Let's try again and see if we can't all act like adults for a change." So we'd go on for another few weeks.

Anyway, this time we weren't kidding. So we all knelt

down beside Mummy's bed. We said the Lord's Prayer together and then Dad prayed:

"O God, we thank you for Anne. We're
sorry she's gone with you now. We don't like
it. We don't like it at all. But you did give her
to us. She's brought much happiness to us.
She was great fun. She was a lovely spirit. She
did more for us than we ever did for her. We
knew she was never far from you, even when
she was with us. We would like to believe now
that somehow it's best for everybody—for us
as well as for her—that she is now with you
completely . . . Keep us close to one another,
God. Thanks for bringing Mummy back safely
home again. We thank you for each other, and

thank you for our friend, Jesus, your Son. May
he stay close to Anne. Amen."

Then we all said, "Amen."

Dad stood up. I looked at him. I can remember thinking,
"He looks older."

Then I looked at Mummy, Her eyes were puffy and red,
and I thought, "It's funny. She looks prettier."

Then I looked out the window, and I saw Bonnie racing
across the street. "Look," I said, "there's Bonnie. He's running
away. Let's go get him."

So Pete, Sally, and I raced down the stairs. As we reached
the bottom, we heard Mummy say, "Don't forget to put your
jackets on." Mummy was back home on the job.

# 8

WE HAD HAMBURGERS AGAIN for lunch that day. Sally cooked them. Mother said she would order a steak for dinner that night and cook it herself. As it turned out, though, she didn't have to. As a matter of fact, nobody in our house had to cook any meals for several days. Meals came in for us. By the end of the afternoon they had begun to come from neighbors and friends—almost in truckloads, it seemed.

Shortly after lunch Dad said, "Okay, kids, get your jackets. We're going to take a walk. All of us. Your mother needs some rest, and we need to get some fresh air."

"Can Bonnie come?" I asked.

"Of course he can," he replied. "He's part of the family, isn't he?"

I knew he didn't expect an answer because we all knew by this time that Bonnie was part of the family.

He hadn't run away far that morning, just across the street chasing a cat. It was the only bad habit he had. He loved to chase cats. Sometimes he snapped at dogs, but he always growled and barked at cats. And every time he chased a cat, it seemed as though the cats would always run across the street. So I told him, "Sometime, Bonnie, old boy, you're going to get in trouble running across the street. A cat is going to take you right in front of a car someday, and you're going to get hit, and that will be the end of you. Now, you stop it. Do you understand?"

He would look up at me with his brown eyes as though he were going to say, "Of course I understand. Of course. I promise never to do it again. But you just don't understand about cats, old Danny boy."

I guess I didn't because the next time a cat came along, he'd do the same thing all over again. In everything else he seemed to have good sense, but with cats no sense at all.

Anyway, that afternoon we all went for a walk. We got into the car, Sally in front with Dad this time, Pete and Bonnie and me in the back seat. Dad drove us out to the state park. There we walked over one of the old mountain trails where we used to go sometimes for a picnic early in the summer. Now it was December. No snow had come yet, but the ground was frozen hard, and it was crisp and clear and bright. We scuffed along through the leaves that had piled up, and they made a nice crunchy sound.

Bonnie was great that afternoon. He would run along sniffing with his nose to the ground. If he left the trail and went down a side path, we'd have to run after him and call him back. Then he'd fall into line for awhile and trot along as we climbed to the top of the mountain. We started walking along the ridge path until it wound down on the other side and then circled back by the base of the mountain to where the car was. Every once in a while Bonnie would tear off. We'd tear off after him and call him back. We had a real workout that afternoon.

Once Pete asked, "Do you think dogs go to heaven, Dad?"

"If they don't," he answered, "then I don't want to go there myself."

"Are we all going to go to heaven?" Sally then asked.

"Well, I don't know whether we all go to heaven or not," Dad answered, "but we all are going to die. That's for sure."

Pete said, "Well, if you don't go to heaven, then where do you go?"

"Beats me," answered Dad. That was a phrase he had picked up from Pete. He kept telling Pete not to use such a silly phrase, and here he was using it himself.

Sally said, "I wonder what it's like in heaven."

"I suppose nobody really knows," Dad replied. "It's not so much a place anyway, you know. It's not like a football field or a baseball diamond, only a million times bigger.

"It's not really a place," he continued. "It's more like being with people. It's especially like being with people that you love all the time. Now, if you're with people you love all the time, that's heaven. Where that takes place doesn't make so much difference."

"What do they do in heaven?" I asked.

"I don't know," said Dad. "I've never been there. I can't say what heaven is absolutely, but I can in part. Heaven is where God is, or rather where he is fully in control; where he's king, top dog. We say 'heaven on earth' when he has his way with us, like when we really love people—that's heaven. Well, in heaven—or when you're with God completely—you love completely and easily all the time. That's why when people describe heaven they use words like *praise* and *glory* and *honor* and *love* and *majesty* and everything that's the greatest."

"I don't get it," I said.

"I know," Dad replied. "It's not easy. In fact it's full of mystery. I don't get it all myself, but hang on for a while. Maybe we'll all get more of it as we talk.

"One thing I do know," he went on, "is that you can't be a lone wolf in heaven. You can't even be a lone wolf here. You belong to other people, and they belong to you. The whole point of living is that you're with people and that you love people and some love you, and you try to be a decent guy.

When you're in heaven you just do this perfectly all the time rather than in the half-baked way we do it here."

"What about wings?" I said. "People are supposed to have wings in heaven, aren't they? Do you suppose Anne has wings?"

Sally piped up, "Yes, what about wings, Dad? How do you get wings? Do they just grow?"

"They're supposed to grow about where the shoulder blades are, aren't they? They're sort of like arms coming out backwards. In some pictures it looks to me as though angels have forward arms and then backward arms."

"Yes, but Anne hasn't got any arms at all, has she?" I asked. "They're going to burn those arms off. They're going to burn her all up. Isn't that right, Dad? How can she fly if she hasn't got any arms?"

"Well, I don't know exactly, Dan. I suppose it's just that

she has a different kind of body now. It's not like her old one, like ours. It's not just simple flesh and blood. It's a new one. Her spirit is what makes it. That spirit which she had here is what *she* is. It comes from God originally. It's God's spirit of love. The body she has now is made up of that.

"The point of saying she has wings is that she isn't just like her old self, but she now lives in a better, new world. It's a spiritual world. That's why heaven is like loving. If all you are is spirit and that spirit is love you can't help loving all the time. You don't have to be a stinker every once in a while the way we are here.

"We all know what it is like to be a stinker," he went on. "I am sometimes. Remember that time I kicked you part way up the stairs, Pete? I was a real stinker then. At least I told you later I was sorry. You are a stinker sometimes. We all are at some time or other."

"Mummy isn't," said Sally.

"Oh yes she is," said Pete. "She clipped me once right on the side of my head. It was when she found out I was lying about where I'd been."

Dad said, "Well, I don't know. She's not much of a stinker, but every once in a while she's a little bit of one."

"Yes," I said. "Just like every morning when she tells us to be sure to put our jackets on and be sure to put our gloves on and be sure to put our mufflers on and don't forget our boots."

"The point is," Dad continued, "simply that she and the rest of us aren't great lots of times. But another point just as important is that lots of times we are great, too. And when we are—when we really love each other—then that's what we're really like when we're with God all the time. When we're with God fully—with no holds barred—like Anne is now, then we're in heaven. That's about all I know. Now, do you get this?"

I said, "Yes, I guess so. When God says 'this is the way it's going to be,' then this is the way it's going to be."

"What you mean," Pete said, "the way I get it, is that in heaven God is the boss all the time, and here on earth he is willing not to be some of the time. Is that right?"

"Yes," said Dad. "Except that when he says 'this is the way it's going to be' we're happy to say in heaven, 'yes, this is the way it's going to be.' When we're our best selves even on earth, this is the way we want it, too. We know then that the way he wants it is the best way for all of us. It's got to be right because it's his. It's going to be the best for the whole bunch of us, including Anne. So we say, 'Okay, God.'"

"Sure," said Pete. "We say, 'Thanks God—thanks a whole

lot for killing Anne.' Not me. I don't. I think it was a dirty trick."

"No," said Dad. "He didn't kill her. But he didn't stop her from dying either. That's what makes it so tough. And that's also what makes it so good, too. Get it?"

"Nope," said Pete. "I don't."

"Neither do I," said Sally.

"Me neither," I said.

Just then Bonnie tore off on another track of his own. He dashed through the underbrush, and the three of us tore after him. He had smelled something, and this time we had an awful job getting him to come back on the trail.

Finally we did, but not until we were almost back to the car. I was pooped. So was Bonnie. On the way home he snuggled up in my arms and put his head on my shoulder and fell asleep. That was neat, I thought, the way he did that. I liked it. I fell asleep, too.

WHEN WE WENT IN through the back door we found Aunt Dorothy in the kitchen sorting out the food. She was Dad's sister and had driven a hundred miles that afternoon after Mummy had called her about Anne. The food was stacked all over the sink and the table and on the floor. It seemed to us that everybody we'd ever known had left something: salads, hams, chickens, casseroles, puddings, cakes, pies, cider, doughnuts, and I don't know what else. I never saw so much food in one place in all my life. For the next couple of days whenever Sally and I answered the doorbell, we would make bets on what the next food was going to be.

Dad said it was simply wonderful the way people brought in whole meals for a family. He said they'd brought in everything except food for breakfast.

"Why doesn't anybody ever bring in food for breakfast," I asked.

Pete said, "It's because everybody wants to be sure we will eat cold cereal."

"Very funny, Pete," Dad said.

That night, though, we didn't have to worry about cold cereal or anything else. What we had was a feast. We ate as we hadn't eaten since that awful business began with Mummy going into the hospital. Aunt Dorothy was a great addition to our household. She put the meals together, and every one was like a surprise picnic.

That night I went in to kiss Mummy and said how glad we were that she was back. She ruffled my hair and said how happy she was that she had us and that she was with us. Then I went upstairs to the top floor and got into bed and was ready for Dad's reading some more of *The Wind in the Willows*. He usually read to me when he was going to be home in the evening. He'd been reading this to me off and on for about six months.

When he came up and sat down on the edge of the bed, I said to him, "There's one thing that still bothers me. If Anne hasn't got a body, how can she love anybody, and how can anybody love her? How does she get around?"

"I didn't say she doesn't have *any* body," Dad replied. "What I said was her body now isn't like the bodies we have—it is not a physical body.

"You don't always need a body, you know," he went on, "to know that you are loved. For instance, lots of times I go away on trips. My body isn't anywhere around here when I'm gone. You can't see me or hear me or touch me. Yet you know that the most important thing about me and you is that I love you—even if I am a miserable character sometimes and clip you when I ought not to. Still you know that the one important thing that you can always count on most is that I love you. Follow me?"

"Yes, I follow you."

"Well, then, this means that you don't need a body to know that. It's not my body that loves you. It's my spirit that keeps on loving you. That's *me* loving you. That spirit of mine which loves you and your spirit is more important than my body or your body. No matter where the bodies might be— whether I'm here or in San Francisco—what you can always count on is that we love each other. Are you still with me?"

"Yes, I'm with you."

"Well, it's the same thing with Anne and God and you and

me and love. It's for keeps. It's for always. Whether you have a body or you don't have a body. The one thing that always keeps on is love. And that's God. And nothing can destroy that no matter what. So neither can Anne be destroyed, nor you nor me. Now, do you think you get this?"

"Yes. Thanks, Dad. I get it. Now, let's find out what stupid old Toad does next."

So he leaned over and opened *The Wind in the Willows* and began to read. I guess I must haven fallen right off to sleep because the next morning I couldn't remember what the foolish thing was that old Toad had done after he got out of jail.

# 9

SOMEHOW THE FUNERAL didn't seem very important. What I mean is that the funeral itself didn't make anything different. It was just part of everything going on during those days. When it was over it was like a chapter of a book was over. There had been something going on before, and there was something going on afterwards. It didn't change things so much as it just said them.

Right at the head of the center aisle in the church there was a box—so close we could almost reach out and touch it. But that box didn't seem to have anything to do with Anne. Men carried it in; they carried it out; the minister raised his hand over it; but we all knew Anne wasn't there. She was too big for any old box to hold. She was in heaven, and she was with God, and she was safe, and she was all right. I think we all agreed on that.

The best thing about the service was the hymns. We sang "Jesus, tender Shepherd, hear me" because Mummy said it reminded her of her mother who had taught it to her. Sally and Pete wanted a happy hymn so the minister chose an Easter one, "The strife is o'er, the battle done." I thought that was a little silly because Anne had never had any strife except at the end when she was sick. Anyway, everybody sang their heads off. It was almost as though they wanted to be sure Anne heard them. Even Dad sang "I sing a song of the saints of God" with all his might. I think, though, maybe he was doing it for us rather than for Anne.

While the funeral was nothing special, the thing that did

make a difference was the party afterwards at the house. Oh, it wasn't a real party like a birthday party. We didn't play games. There weren't any prizes, though there were refreshments. But it was a party in the sense that there was something good going on, and you were part of it. It was a nice, deep, safe feeling that was around the house.

There were lots of people there—relatives came from all over; lots of neighbors and friends; people we had never seen before, but who had come hundreds of miles because they were friends of Dad and Mummy's.

Some cousins and some of our friends came. There were punch and cookies for the children out on the side porch. We would go out there; we'd eat something; and then we'd wander back into the living room. There was a lot of coming and going.

Some of the people talked in little groups. Some people didn't say anything. They just came in; most of them would kiss Mummy and shake hands with Dad. Sometimes they'd put their arms around one or the other of them. Something good was going on. It didn't have very much to do with the words that were said. It was more just something in the air—something strong and gentle at the same time.

I remember, though, standing near my uncle once and hearing him say to two other people who were there, "The fact is, Anne has already counted for more in her life of two years than I will count in my whole life."

I wasn't sure I knew what he meant, but I thought I did. One of the men said, "We know what you mean." And the other added, "We sure do." It was nice and it made me warm.

And I felt safe.

# 10

SNOW CAME the week after Christmas. It stayed until the end of March. The cold came, too. It was the cold that killed Bonnie. He froze to death, and that is what I've got to tell now.

It was on Washington's birthday night that I let Bonnie out after supper. For some reason he just took off like a streak. I didn't see any cat, but there must have been one. He tore across the street and off into the darkness faster than I'd ever seen him go before. Though I ran after him and called and called, he just disappeared.

It had been snowing all day long. Because of the snow and

because of the holiday there was almost no traffic. I thought that was lucky because then there wouldn't be so much chance of his getting run over. I walked up and down the main street where he had run. Buses with chains on would go by once in a while moving very slowly. The clinking of those chains was almost the only noise. I stayed out about an hour looking for him until I was almost frozen. Then both Pete and Dad went out and looked for him.

Finally Dad said, "Look, Dan, you can't stay out here all night. We'll each take one more turn around the neighborhood, and then we'll meet back at the house. If we still haven't found him, then you'll have to go to bed anyway."

"Can't we call the police?" I asked.

"No," he said, "we can't call the police at this hour of the night about a dog. But if he hasn't shown up by morning, we'll call the dog pound, and then I'll call the police.

So we combed the neighborhood once more. Still no Bonnie.

When we got back to the house, Dad said, "All right. Now that's all. You've got to go to bed. I'll go out again once more later tonight before I go to bed, and you can get up early in the morning if you want to."

"Well," I said, "I'm going to leave his banket and some bones out here by the back door, just in case he comes home during the night."

"Okay, that's a good idea, but just shake a leg."

So I put the blanket outside the back door where he usually came in and placed some dog bones on it. Then I went upstairs and went to bed and asked God to please bring Bonnie back. Finally—it seemed hours later—I fell asleep.

The next morning I got up before the rest of the family,

dressed, and went downstairs. On the hall table was a note from Dad:

> Dan, I have just been out again. No sign of Bonnie. If you go out early to look for him, don't forget to come back in time for breakfast before you go to school.
>
> > *Love,*
> > *Dad*
>
> 1 A.M.

I put on my jacket and muffler and hat and gloves and boots. Mother didn't have to remind me because it was ten degrees above zero. When I went out it was freezing, and there was a new light cover of snow over everything. There was no traffic.

I found him two blocks from the house. He was lying in the snow between the sidewalk and the curb. He was lying on one side. Almost all of him was covered with snow, except his face and left paw were sticking out, brown and clear against the snow—and stiff and frozen.

I tried to lift him, but I couldn't bear the touch of his cold fur and knew I could never carry him all the way back in my arms. So I ran home, picked up his blanket, which was outside the back door, and shook off the snow. I brought it back and put it down on the snow next to him. Then, trying hard not to look too closely, I pushed him with my foot onto the blanket. Finally, I got him into the middle. Then I picked up the four corners and dragged him home to the back door. I didn't know what to do with him then, so I left him in the snow and went inside.

Mother was making breakfast, and she said, "Any sign of him?"

"Yes. I found him. He was out in front of the Connellys' by the curbstone. Dead."

"Oh, Danny, what happened?"

"I don't know. He must have been hit by a bus. He probably dragged himself up on the sidewalk and was trying to get back home, but couldn't make it and froze to death. Or maybe somebody saw him get hit and carried him out of the street and put him on the curb and left him there. Then he froze to death."

"Oh, Danny, where is he now?"

"He's outside. I can't bring him in. . . . Oh, Mother, I think I'm going to be sick."

"Come on in quickly to the bathroom."

So I went in and I threw up. I felt awful. Just awful. Then I cried.

WHEN I CAME OUT, Dad was downstairs. He said, "Never mind, now, Dan, about Bonnie. You leave him to me. I'll take care of him and see that everything is all right. You don't have to do another thing. You've done enough, and you've been a good egg." He gave me a nice gentle pat on the side of the head, the way he does when he's pleased.

"As a matter of fact, you don't even have to go to school this morning if you don't want to."

"No," I said, "I'll go. I might as well go." I was surprised to hear myself say it.

I didn't eat much breakfast. Mother made me drink a cup of tea, and I had a piece of toast. Then I went to school out through the front door.

When I got home from school in the afternoon, Mother was in the kitchen. She made me some hot chocolate, and I sat down at the kitchen table.

After a while I asked, "Mummy, what are we going to do with all those things of Bonnie's?"

She replied, "Never mind now. I've picked them all up downstairs and stored them away in a box. They are all down there in the cellar—that is, everything except the collar." She took the collar out of the kitchen table drawer and gave it to me.

"Here," she said, "I thought maybe you'd like to keep this up in your room. Someday you're going to have another dog, and then we can get all the other things out again."

"Maybe I will some day," I said, "but not now."

"That's right," she said. "Some day but not now. It wouldn't be right to have another dog—not now anyway."

"I know it. I don't want one. I don't want one to take his place anyway. He was a member of the family, and you can't just have somebody else come and take somebody else's place. That's his own place."

"No," she said. "You're dead right. You can't. You just can't. Nobody can take anybody's place for him." Her eyes began to fill with tears. I looked away and asked, "What did Dad do with him?"

"I don't know," she replied. "He called the dog pound. They came and took him away. But," she went on, "it doesn't really make any difference what they have done with his body. Bonnie was Bonnie, no matter where they took his body or what they did to it. He'll always be a part of us wherever we go."

"I know it," I said. Then I thought, "Well, this is just the same with Anne. No matter what happened to her body she will always be a part of us, no matter where we go, too."

I started to say this to Mother, but then I thought, "That's silly. If I know it, then she knows it already."

Then she said, "What're you going to do now, Danny?"

"I don't know," I said. "I think I'll take Bonnie's collar and put it upstairs on my desk, and maybe I'll take a little snooze."

And that is what I did.

# 11

EASTER CAME EARLY THIS YEAR. It was five weeks after Bonnie was killed.

On the way home from church Sally said, "You know, Danny, we never had a funeral for Bonnie. Why don't you and I put one together for the family—not a real funeral, but kind of a memorial service?"

"Great," I said. "That's a neat idea. Let's find out when everybody is going to be home today." Aunt Dorothy and Uncle Tom were visiting us. So we asked Dad.

He said that he thought everybody would be home by six o'clock that evening. After dinner Sally and I got to work and spent most of the afternoon making up a service and arranging the living room so that it looked like a church.

There was a cross on a wall in the study upstairs. I took it down and put it on the mantelpiece over the fireplace. Sally took two candles from the sideboard in the dining room and put them on either side of the cross. We changed the furniture around so there was a center aisle up the middle of the living room, and the chairs and sofas became pews. The two biggest chairs we put on either side of the fireplace facing each other. Then I went down cellar and nailed a strip of board crosswise on an old broomstick handle to make a processional cross.

We had a long talk about what we ought to wear. Sally finally decided she would put her best dress back on. I put on her bathrobe. Since she is taller than I am it hung down almost to the floor, so I decided it looked enough like a robe that the minister wears in church for it to be Okay.

By six o'clock everyone had come home. We ushered them to their seats—Mother and Dad, Pete, Aunt Dorothy and Uncle Tom. Joey and the twins from next door happened to come in about that time, and since they were good friends, we invited them in, too.

Sally first lit the candles. Then I announced from the hallway that the first hymn would be "Jesus Christ is risen today." We had forgotten to ask Mummy to play the piano, but she got up and went over to it, and we got started. Sally led the way down the center aisle carrying the cross, and I brought up the rear in her bathrobe. We took our places in front of the fireplace. She stood in front of one arm chair and I in front of the other. We finished the hymn.

"The service will begin," I said, "with Sally reading a prayer. When she finishes, we'll all join in the Lord's Prayer."

Sally then read this prayer:

O Merciful Father, whose face the angels of thy little ones do always behold in heaven; Grant us steadfastly to believe that this thy dog, Bonnie, hath been taken into the safe keeping of thine eternal love; through Jesus Christ our Lord. Amen.

After that we said the Lord's Prayer together.

"The Scripture Lesson comes next," I said, "and it is going to be Psalm 23:

The LORD is my shepherd; I shall not want.

He maketh me to lie down in green pastures: he leadeth me beside the still waters.

He restoreth my soul: he leadeth me in the paths of righteousness for his name's sake.

Yea, though I walk through the valley of the shadow of death, I will fear no evil: for thou art with me; thy rod and thy staff they comfort me.

Thou preparest a table before me in the presence of mine enemies: thou anointest my head with oil; my cup runneth over.

Surely goodness and mercy shall follow me all the days of my life: and I will dwell in the house of the LORD for ever.

"Now we have the sermon," I said. "It goes like this." I pretended to read from a sheet of paper, but I already knew what I wanted to say.

"God gives dogs to children," I began. "He gives them so they can be friends. It's just like he gives children to parents so they can be friends, too.

"Sometimes after he gives dogs for a while he takes them back again. I don't know why he does this, unless it's because he loves them and wants to play with them himself. Maybe he needs friends, too.

"The same thing happens sometimes with children, too. They go away from us and go to live with him.

"Some day, though, we'll all be together—dogs and children and parents—and then we'll live happily ever after.

"That's the end of the sermon."

Then I forgot what was supposed to happen next, so I whispered to Sally, "What are we supposed to do now?"

She said, "The collection."

"Oh. Yes," I went on. "Next comes another hymn. It's

going to be 'I sing a song of the saints of God.'" I looked at Dad. He winked at me.

Then I said, "During the singing of the hymn, we will take up the collection." Dad started to laugh, but stopped when Aunt Dorothy looked at him.

I forgot to say that Sally had taken a plate from the kitchen and put it on the mantelpiece to serve as a collection plate. While we sang the hymn, I passed it around.

After we had sung the doxology, I said, "Now we will kneel for the benediction." And then I read:

> Unto God's gracious mercy and protec-
> tion we commit you. The Lord bless you and
> keep you. The Lord make his face to shine
> upon you, and be gracious unto you. The Lord

lift up his countenance upon you, and give you
peace, both now and evermore. Amen.


"The recessional hymn is 'My country 'tis of thee,'" I announced. Sally picked up the cross, I picked up the collection
plate, and we marched out. She went back and blew out the
candles and then came up the stairs to the landing to help me
count the money.

When the family came out, Dad looked up at us and asked,
"Well, how much was it?"

"There's a dollar and eighty-seven cents," I said, "and a
ten dollar bill from Uncle Tom. That's eleven eighty-seven."

"What are you going to do with all that money?" he asked.

"I'm going to give it to the minister for some worthy
cause," I replied. I looked down at Mother and Dad. I thought

for a moment that Mummy was about to burst into tears and Dad into laughter. But neither one did.

I gave the money to the minister that week, and later he wrote me a nice two-page letter in his own handwriting thanking me for the money. He said that he was sending it to a friend of his who was a missionary in Japan.

So that was the end of the funeral service for Bonnie.

# 12

IT WASN'T UNTIL THIS SUMMER that we buried Anne—that is, that we buried her ashes. We were going back to the beach for our summer vacation. I said I wanted to hold the box that had her ashes in my lap.

Dad said, "No, that's not necessary. But we'll put you in the back with the luggage, and you can keep an eye on the box." So that settled the matter. We drove down in the station wagon. I sat in the back, and the ashes made the trip with no trouble.

The next day Dad made arrangements with the minister at the beach, who was an old friend of his from school days, to have the burial service. They decided to have it the next day.

There wasn't any regular cemetery at the beach, but the minister said we could use a part of the church grounds that was in a pine grove. That pleased everybody. The minister and Dad and Mummy and the three of us walked all over the area, and finally we decided on a place on the side of a slope. There was nothing there except ground covering, bayberry bushes, and pine trees. It was a little removed from the church, but there was a nice path that went right by it.

That afternoon Dad and Pete dug a hole for the box to fit into. Sally and I nailed together a wooden cross. We used thumbtacks to put Anne's initials on it, together with the two dates of her birth and death. This was going to mark the grave until we got a regular grave marker.

Dad and Mummy had decided that it would be a very

simple service with just a few close friends there. I asked Dad if I could ask Mr. Field and his wife to come. He replied, "Of course, Dan, I should have thought of that myself. Why don't you go down and ask them?"

So I went down the road where the sand dobbies used to come out and play with Mr. Field and on up to his house. I knocked on the door, and he opened it.

"Hello, Dan," he said, "I'm delighted to see you. Won't you come in?" And he stepped aside and, with a little blow, welcomed me in.

I stepped in and said, "I just came down to say that we're going to bury Anne's ashes tomorrow morning, and we'd all love it if you and Mrs. Field could come."

"Why, Dan, I'm sure we are honored to be asked. Of course we'll come. What time shall we be there?"

"Ten o'clock."

"Thank you for asking us. We'll be there. Won't you sit down?"

"No," I said, "I think I'd better be going back."

He walked part way back down the road with me past the sand-dobby place. I wanted to ask him if he'd seen many sand dobbies during the winter, but then I thought maybe he would think it was a childish question, so I didn't say anything.

He talked about the trip he and Mrs. Field had taken during the winter to Greece and how the light there was almost as clear and sharp and bright as it was at the beach. He said the best thing for him was the light and the water and the way they kept changing all the time. "Very wonderful," he said, "and very mysterious."

Then as he shook my hand good-by, he said, "You know what? I've learned something more about sand dobbies this year."

"You have? What?"

"Well, I discovered that they're everywhere. They're not just in one or two or three places at certain times, you know, the way we've seen them sometimes down at the fork in the road. Oh, they may be there, of course—that is, they do come out, and at certain times and certain places we human beings can see them best. That's just where they're visible.

"But they're invisible, too. That's maybe the most important thing I found out all winter long, Dan. They're all around this place all the time, only you can't see them. They're in and out of the trees, and they're in and out of the ocean and on the sand and on the grass, and they're in the lakes, and they surround us every minute. I used to believe that they had secret hiding places, but they don't. They're right here all the time."

"Well, what do they do?" I asked.

"Do? They don't *do* anything. They just *are*. Isn't that extraordinary? Don't you think it would be great just to be and not to worry about doing things all the time?"

"Yes, I guess so. Sure, that is." I wasn't quite sure what he meant, but whatever it was was very important to him, for he spoke very slowly.

"Sand dobbies," he said, "live in and out of trees so that the trees can be trees. They are what make trees trees. They live in and around and above bushes so that bushes can be bushes. They live on hillsides so that hillsides can be hillsides. They're in lakes so that lakes can be lakes. They're in the green color of the grass so that green can be green. They make red berries red. They are whatever *is*; they hold all things together; and they make things just be whatever they are—birds or water or color or sand or beach, grass or whatever.

"Sand dobbies teach us to be just ourselves, I think. Not

to try all the time to go do things but to be whatever we are; to accept ourselves the way we are; to accept everything that happens so that we can be a part of everything that happens.

"Sand dobbies say, 'Don't try to be somebody else. Don't try to change other people. You be yourself and let everybody else be themselves.' At least that's the way they seem to me.

"Even when death comes," he went on, "let it come. It's part of life." He stopped and looked at me. "Do you follow me, Dan?"

"You mean about Anne?" I asked.

"Yes, about Anne. She's part of life. She *is* life, you might say. She was Anne, wasn't she, just because she was Anne? Not particularly because she did anything. Doing things was just the visible part of her. When she died, she stopped doing things visibly for us; but the real Anne—the real person, the sand-dobby part of her—why, that didn't die, that goes on because she still *is*. She is still part of life and of everything that is, because she herself still is.

"Seeing sand dobbies is the same as being able to see people because they have bodies. But even when you can't see their bodies any more the sand-dobby part of them-—the *real* part—still goes on.

"So," he ended, "don't you ever forget about sand dobbies. See you tomorrow." And he shook my hand just as though I were a grownup.

# 13

THE SERVICE THE NEXT MORNING was nice and simple. The box with Anne's ashes was on the altar and a cloth placed over it. The minister read from the Bible and had a prayer.

Then he said, "Now I want to say just one word. This is a terrible thing—for a lovely two-year-old girl to die. She never hurt anybody; she didn't do anything except bring pleasure to people; and she did it simply because she *was*."

I could see Mother tighten her hand, and Dad put his hand over hers. I thought, "I'll bet they don't want him to do any more talking." But he went on anyway. Then as he continued they began to relax.

"I don't like it," he said. "You don't like it. Nobody likes it. We all really hate it. We hate death. I'd like to tell God where to get off for letting this happen. Maybe you already have. I hope you have."

Well, I had. I had told God, "You are a stinker." I don't know whether he liked it or not, but that's the way I felt. And more than that, I had a feeling that God was kind of pleased to have me speak to him like that. He certainly understood. Anyway, I liked what this man was saying.

"But once you've done that," he continued, "then what are you going to do next? You're not God. We're not God. You can tell him to go to the devil, but he's still God. God is God. *He* just is. Even if he didn't *do* anything, he *is* everything.

"He's the very ground we walk on and live in. He's the air we breathe. He's the height and depths. Right down in the bottom of us, he is there. He *is*. There's no place we can go to escape him. We can go out on the water, we can go up in the air, we can go down deep inside ourselves. Wherever we are, he is. Wherever life is, he is. And—and this is the point I want to make—wherever death is, he is too.

"So what you can do—the only thing you can do—is to give him your life and to give him your death. So give him Anne—her life and her death—freely, willingly, and gladly, if you can do it. She's with him. She is in him, and she is all right. Anybody with God is all right. So don't try to hang on to her. You don't own her. She's God's. You can't hold her. What you can do is to give her to God. And if you can do it gracefully, so much the better.

"And if you do, that's when somehow she comes back to live with you. I don't know why this is so, but she becomes a part of you and of life through her death, even more somehow than when she did things in her life here. So if you possibly can, give her freely to God. Then you'll be able to have her to live with as you never had before.

"I think," he said, "that this is simply the way life is. I'm not trying to argue; I'm not trying to persuade anybody; I'm just trying to describe the way things *are*. This is the way I see it.

"God is God. And Jesus is Jesus. If you look at him you can see what I am trying to say. That death of his was just as senseless as Anne's. Actually it was worse, for he was innocent all his life long. He wasn't guilty of sin the way the rest of us are. Yet he died.

"God used his death to show everybody in the world how much he loved them. Jesus was willing to offer himself to God because he loved him and because this was the way God had decided to use him to let us know that he loved us, that the only thing we can count on finally in life is his love for us. In life and in *death,* God is still God. He is the father of Jesus, and he is our father.

"The point in Jesus's life was that he lived in response to God. That means in response to love. It was love that controlled his life. When we respond to love—especially when we let it control us—then we belong to that world where God is in absolute control. And the way he extends his control on the earth is as we love one another and offer ourselves to his control.

"So when we offer Anne to God, we can believe that Jesus says, 'All is well with Anne' because we know that all is well with people who are with him. We then can get on with our primary business, which is living right here and being ourselves right here and trying to love a little bit better than we have before. It is to live with a little bit more joy and a little bit more happiness, to sing a little bit more, not to be so exercised by the things of this world because we know that we belong to another world finally. Anne is in that world. God is there. We'll be there. So let us get on with living and loving, which is the business of life, and thank God for everything. Especially Anne. Amen."

Gee, I thought, that was pretty good. I think everybody else did, too. Anyway, a real load seemed to have been lifted from everybody. Nobody seemed to be very sad as we then walked down the hill. The minister carried Anne's ashes and placed them in the hole that Dad and Pete had dug. He asked Pete to shovel in some dirt while he said, "earth to earth, ashes to ashes, dust to dust."

When he had finished Pete stuck in the cross that we had made. Then the minister said, "Let's say the Lord's Prayer together." So we did that, and when that was over everybody shook hands. That was nice. I don't know why they did it, but it was real nice.

As we were walking up the hill to where the cars were, Mummy and Dad were ahead, then Pete and Sally followed. Mr. Field was walking next to me. I said to him, "That was nice, wasn't it?"

He said, "It sure was, Dan. Real nice."

We stopped for a minute and looked back over the pine grove and down the slope of the hill where the cross was. I said to Mr. Field, "Do you believe what the minister just said? That part about God being in control of everything? And if we give Anne to him she comes back to us?"

"Well," he said, "that's his language, and it's good language, too. My language is more like sand-dobby language, but I think we're both saying the same thing. Yes," he said, then turning to me, "I believe what he said."

"Mr. Field," I asked, "what are we going to see when we die?"

"Why," he replied, "when I die I'm going to see the face of God. What are you going to see?"

"Well, I don't know. I guess I am, too. I never thought of it just like that. I like that—that seeing the face of God. Maybe we'll see the sand dobbies then, too. Do you think we will?"

"Dan," he replied, "I'm sure we will. What's heaven without sand dobbies to go along with dogs and children and people loving each other?"

We turned around and walked to the car. When we reached it, he shook hands once more and turned to walk with his wife. He looked serious, and he had a smile at the same time. I loved him.

In the car on the way back to the cottage we sang songs. Usually, the only time we'd sing songs was at beach picnics around the campfire in the dark. But this time we sang, "Old MacDonald Had a Farm," "She'll Be Comin' Round the Mountain When She Comes," "He Told Her He Loved Her, But Oh, How He Lied," and "Lord Jeffrey Amherst." Nobody in our family went to Amherst, but it was the only college song everybody knew.

Just as we drove into the driveway, I said, "You know, when I think of God now, I think of Anne. And when I think of Anne, I think of God. Do you think it's all right if I pray to Anne sometimes instead of God, even though I know she's not God?"

"Of course it's all right," said Dad. "You can't keep the two apart, and if it helps to see Anne with God, then do it. Certainly."

"Well, what about Jesus, Dad?" asked Pete. "What are you going to do about him?"

"I don't know," he replied. "I'm not going to do anything about him. I know he's around there with God and Anne. And he's around there just to be with her. He is *for* her the way he is for us. And if she's having a good time, he is. Or maybe it's the other way around: since he is having a good time, she is, too. So I'm not going to worry about him."

Then, thinking of the way Mr. Field had turned my question back to me, I asked, "Pete what are you going to do about him?"

"Beats me," he said, as he got out of the car.

Dad said, "For heaven's sake, Pete, that is half-baked language to use. Why does he do it, Jean, anyway?"

"Beats me," she said.

Then we went into the house, put on our bathing suits, and ran to the beach.

# 14

IT WAS THE NEXT TO THE LAST DAY of vacation. We were all lying on the beach. Sally and Pete were talking about the last dance they were going to that night. Mummy was reading. Dad was lying on his stomach with his head on his arms.

I was sitting up looking down the beach when I spotted a dog trotting along. He reminded me of Bonnie, although he was bigger.

To nobody in particular I said, "You know, I think it would be nice to have a dog again."

Mummy said, "If you want one, Danny, and your father says it's all right, then I think you ought to have one."

"What about it, Dad? Do you think I can have a dog?"

Dad said, "Certainly you can have a dog. You can have one on your next birthday and start all over again."

"Oh," said Mummy, "don't make the boy wait another three months. Remember how long that was for him to wait last year?"

Dad said, "You're right, Jean. I was only kidding. You're right. You always are. At least you're always right when it comes to dogs—dogs and little children and things like that."

Mummy said, "Children aren't things, dear. Neither are dogs."

"I know it," he said. "They're lovely, lovely animals, and we're happy to have them. They're great. The salt of the earth.

They keep you humble, annoyed, and happy. We like both dogs and children."

"Oh, for heaven's sake," Mummy said, "that's no way to talk."

Dad laughed, and turning to me he said, "Dan, what kind of a dog do you want? You decide the one you want and we'll get it as soon as we go home. We'll buy any dog you want— providing it's within reason, of course."

"Well," I said, "I'd sort of like to try the dog pound again. Is that Okay?"

"Of course it's Okay. That's even a better idea."

As he stood up, he clipped me alongside the ear. "Come on," he said, "I'll beat you into the water." But *I* beat him. That was cool.

THREE DAYS LATER I got a collie at the dog pound. We named him Bonnie II. I have had him now almost three months. One of the best things about him is that he doesn't chase cats. He barks at them and scares them. He has never run away, and I hope he never does.